CONTENT

Unless otherwise stated, all scriptural quotations are from the King James Version of the bible.

KEYS TO OTHER TRANSLATIONS USED

NKJV   -   NEW KING JAMES VERSION

NIV   -   NEW INTERNATIONAL VERSION

AMP   -   THE AMPLIFIED BIBLE

NLT   -   NEW LIVING TRANSLATION

QUOTATION AND PHILOSOPHIES BY, (KEYS TO NAMES)

AD   - ADROIT (AUTHOR).   **RS**   - ROBERT SCHULLER.

TILO – NSIKAK USEN.   **VC**   - VAN DE CAMP.

AL   - ABRAHAM LINCOLN.   **HK**   - HELEN KELLER.

MM   – MIKE MURDOCK   .   **D.A.B** – D.A. BATTISTA.

BD   - BENJAMIN DISREALI.   **ZZ**   - ZIG ZIGLAR.

AOF - AN OLD FRIEND.

DEDICATION

Again, to him who gave me this desire

To him who these thoughts did inspire

To him whose wisdom only I require

By whose strength I will never retire

(THE HOLY GHOST)

Also, to the one I'm bound by fate

Whose own I'm called till date

Whose paps I sucked till late

Who laboured to make me great.

(MY MOTHER)

I dedicate this work to all who wish to excel in life, to the youth who has a dream, to the cause to create the Nigerian dream, to my dear late mother, **Mrs. Helen J.D. Usen**, to my Siblings, **Aniebo Usen, Edidiong Samuel Udoh, Nsikak Usen** and **Iniobong Usen**. To my late father **J.D. Usen**, who never had the guts to apprehend his dreams, to my friend **Karipre Beredugo**, and to the two most important people in my life whom I love with every breath in me: my mentor: The **Lord Jesus** and my dearest friend: **My Queen; whoever she may be.**

INTRODUCTION

Have you ever been depressed? Have you ever felt like you are in the wrong place, living with the wrong people, having the wrong conversations, and even worshipping in the wrong congregation?

Have you ever felt so lonely, so unloved, so betrayed, so distorted you wish you had made some choices in your past differently?

Your lovely family, cherished siblings and well beloved mother keep raising their expectation of you, never once stopping to think how on earth you could ever reach such an Expectation.

The woman you love the most, the man you've buried your heart in, just knows how to set your heart ablaze, and leave you struggling to keep yourself in one piece.

Have you ever stopped to think about your life presently, whether or not you like the outcome? Have you ever asked yourself, *"why am I like this?"*

Perhaps certain laws are working against you; perhaps your destiny doesn't cross paths with the good life. Whatever your thoughts or case may be, you are not alone in it, and you sure can get out of it and be exactly who or what you always dreamt of being. First you have to understand that you are where you are, who you are and what you are by choice, and be ready to *"make changes,"* I realized myself, that I was a product of my own choices, but I never made changes, and so nothing ever really changed. However, when I decided to make changes, I found out I had to stop permitting certain things, in order to change my situation......indeed, you are what you permit.

In life, they are no laws; there are only circumstances and events. If you understand this, then you will comprehend the possibility of breaking laws without breaking rules.

Yes, we actually live by rules and not by laws. We live our lives by a set of conditions which we permit by choice and decision to control us and the circumstances of our lives; conditions we choose to abide by. Rules are actually instructions that impose those conditions on our wills, telling us what we are allowed to do and what we are not allowed to do. Only through freedom can we excel. True freedom comes when we learn to live our lives independent of other people's expectation. Then and only then can we live a fulfilled life, then and only then can we live free of condemnation and disapproval, for of all condemnation and disapproval, that which destroys is self condemnation.

"Your personal convictions...exercise [them] as in God's presence, keeping them to yourself [striving only to know the truth and obey his will]. Blessed (happy, to be envied) is he who has no reason to judge himself (that condemneth not himself) for what he approves (permits) [who does not convict himself by what he chooses to do]." **ROM 14:22 (KJV/AMP HYBRID)**

Learn from Gina's failure: understand Adroit's philosophies.

CHAPTER ONE

<u>GINA'S FAILURE</u>

*"My son, keep thy father's commandment, and forsake not the law of thy mother.....when thou goest, it shall lead thee; when thou sleepest it shall keep thee; and when thou wakest, it shall talk with thee." **PROV 6:20, 22.***

They took to heart their father's words, and fought with it as gallant swords. They all succeeded with great success, except for GINA's great distress. This was the story of ADROIT's seven; this is the story of GINA's failure.

After all her father's advice, and such promising future of uncommon device; GINA thought within herself, why be the one to clean the shelf.

"Why must I be the one to serve, when all his glory I do deserve? Why name me there an associate? I from this name do dissociate. I'll build myself an empire that even father will desire."

Gina sought to start a firm, which she thought will bring her fame. She worked so hard for serious gain, but all she got was grievous pain. She did forget her father's sayings which would have brought her gainful 'payings'.

"Keep going my daughter..." He did say, *"...and you will find good laughter,"*

GINA laboured a couple more years and gathered herself a couple more tears. She faced what she thought her own worst fears, and found she had only foolish cares. So alas! She made up her mind, that her path to true success she must find. She set on course to find her father, and set to all his treasures gather.

"I will return to my father's kingdom, and there I'll relish his every wisdom. I will go fall at his feet, and eat from him philosophical meat,"

GINA picked up her remains, and made sure there were no restrains. She went right to ADROIT's domain where all treasures still contain.

She got to her father's feet on her knees; him she did greet with her pleas.

"Father dear father, I have strayed, and your wisdom I've betrayed"

"No my dear daughter, you have frayed, and your freedom you've delayed" ADROIT answered.

"But I'm glad that you have learnt, since your own wisdom you have spent" ADROIT continued, *"Since by tears you discovered, may all your years be recovered. Come my dear, tell me your fears, and I with care will wipe your tears,"*

GINA spoke forth beneath her wrath,

"Father my fears are, through the years, to be one that men will serve, that I may never deserve. I fear that while I labour for men, all I do may never remain, and while I work and seek to know, I myself will never be known"

She looked up to the glitter ceiling and shook her head in bitter feeling.

"I wish to bear the name: the greatest, and have for me the fame: the dearest. I want to have such wealth untold, and live to have great health unfold. I want to be the merchant's choice and still remain the peasants' voice. I wish to be and have it all, and be the one the world will call,"

She looks into her father's eyes, gnashes her teeth and then she cries.

"I'd love to travel the valiant course, but not as the gallant horse: I'd love to sound the victory throng, but not as the crier's gong: I'd love to time the finer's work, but not as the timer's Clock-Yes I'd love to reach the top but not as the ladder,"

ADROIT wears a very wide smile and stares at Gina for quite a while; picks her up to sit with him and spills out words that sit within.

"A zero after a valued figure gives to it a valued vigour. Fear not then to stand; that zero, for only then you'd to be the hero,"

"Persius was a valiant man, Pegasus was his gallant horse. Though he rose to glorious fame; we only hear of Pegasus' name. Every great finer in London city runs to and fro to make good their dues; the only one person that stands free yet noticed is 'big Ben' the dock that times how they work,"

ADROIT paused and patted his daughter, and then he spoke on his mouth full of laughter.

"No matter how hard the crier may shout, men only listen after the gong sounds. No matter how noisy the top men in town, they'll all need the ladder on their way down. And have not you noticed the ladder's unique? It's still at the bottom and yet at the top."

He nudged his daughter to go to sleep, and when she wakes she'll definitely reap.

"Go eat my daughter and put on some weight, when you have rested we'll rewrite your fate. Go now my daughter and take you your rest, and when you awaken, I'll give you your best."

GINA went and had a meal and gave herself some fill, to sleep, upon her bed she lay until a brand new day.

CHAPTER TWO

<u>ADROIT'S WINNING PHILOSOPHIES</u>

"My son, give attention to my words; incline your ear to my sayings. Do not let them depart from your eyes; keep them in the midst of your heart. For they are life to those who find them and health to all their flesh,"

PROV. 4:20-22 (NKJV)

GINA awoke before the morning sun arose, and rushed to her father as her day's starter. Err' she bids *"good morning"* to her dear folk; he opened his mouth and new words he spoke.

"Listen to me and pay attention; I'll run my mouth free without intention. Listen to me; be careful to hear, for the words I will speak is the wisdom you seek"

At this he stood up from his prayerful knee; turned to his dear daughter as she watched him with glee.

"Take a seat..." He said, *"...and say not a word, for when I am through you'll have a new world."*

At this he breathed deep and took him a seat, and when he was settled, he began words, to spit.

AOF *"The attractions you allow to become distractions cause ungodly actions that leave your salvation in fractions."*

AD *"Know yourself my dear..."* He said, *"...for if you know yourself, there is no limit to what you can achieve."*

TILO "Never my daughter, I say never..." He stressed, "...never underestimate the power of stupid people in large groups"

AD "Write my dear write; it's amazing, what you'll forget, that piece of paper will remember."

AD "Read my dear read, when you so do, you'll extend your lead."

TILO "Remember, if you are not climbing up, you will have nobody looking up to you"

TILO "People will always look up to someone at the top and look down on the person at the bottom. This is an inevitable fact of life,"

"Some facts about failure my dear, keep them in you heart very clear"

AL "It is far more honourable to fail than to cheat."

MM "When you fail to plan; you plan to fail"

TILO "Failure is the evidence that you succeeded in trying"

TILO "If you fail, it is because you tried; if you try again, it is because you didn't fail"

BD "And never admit failure until you've made your last attempt. Never make your last attempt until you've succeeded"

Adroit bid his daughter, "go, get refreshed and when you have freshened, go ahead get dressed. When you are all set, fix us a meal, and after we have eaten, more I'll reveal,"

ADROIT enjoyed his meal of barbecue and stew, and when he was due, he was thankful not a few. But while the meats between his lips; of wine, taking gentle sips; graceful words he kept on giving, and left his daughter simply beaming.

TILO & AD *"I once had a vision that became my conviction..."* he said, biting into a barbecue,

"...then it became my mission, decision and recognition..." he took a sip of fine wine,

"...now it has become my agitation, for I must see yet another vision or I shall become to all nation yet another extinction,"

"But then..." he said, taking another bite, TILO *"...Nobody goes forward looking back."*

"Some thoughts you must bear in mind; they will definitely keep your kind."

TILO *"'I have arrived' is the language of fools, failures and dead men"*

TILO *"Your weakness is actually your strength used against you."*

TILO *"Think about the past: you are frustrated. Think about the present: you are depressed. Think about the future: you are focused."*

TILO *"The sweetest revenge you can give to those who think you a failure is to succeed."*

Reclining on his dinning seat and wiping his mouth, he says, looking away from her,

TILO *"Only great men take little things seriously."*

Suddenly he looked intently at her, as though she sat considerably afar, and began to speak words without pause as one hasty to run a course.

RS *"Success is a journey not a destination"*

RC *"Winners are just ex-losers who got mad,"*

HK "The most pathetic person in this world is someone who has sight but no vision"

TILO "If you want to be poor, look for someone to blame for all your problems. If you want to be rich, blame yourself"

TILO "If the head sympathizes with the tail they both make no progress, if you regard those who are with you at the bottom, you will never succeed."

TILO "Sudden wealth is suddenly gone if not suddenly managed."

TILO "He who knows where he is going will lead, but he who does not know where he is going will follow,"

TILO "Opportunities often come as problems and seldom as solutions."

TILO "What keeps you where you are is the mistake of regarding what should be discarded and discarding what should be regarded,"

He stood up silently, his eyes still fixed on Gina.

D.A.B "The scars you acquire while exercising courage..." he said standing,

"...will never make you inferior."

TILO "Take a man of vision to an Island of nothing and he'll make something out of it. Take a man without vision to an Island of something and he'll make nothing out of it."

"You know my daughter..." he said,

TILO "...It's no news to me when a pauper suddenly attains great wealth, but it's a shocking news when a wealthy man suddenly becomes a pauper. I wonder: 'how did a pauper manage to disguise as a wealthy man for so long?'"

"Wow! Our time is far spent; we must engage ourselves in other businesses of the day"

ADROIT wondered aloud,

"But then, never ever dispel this thought..."

He said to her,

TILO "the success calls the past: experience, the present: opportunity and the future: vision. The failure calls the past: circumstance, the present: predicament and the future: whatever-will-be-will-be."

At this, he walked away.

CHAPTER THREE

7 ATTRIBUTES OF SUCCESS

"Meditate on these things; give yourself entirely to them (throw yourself wholly to them), that your progress (profit, success) may appear (be evident) to all (everybody)"

1 TIM 4:15 (KJV/NKJV/AMP HYBRID)

God, Gold and Glory: This was the story of Adroit's life. Baffled, brass and bewildered: this was the story of Gina's strife. Alas! For her a kingdom was near, she made a choice: wisdom to hear. So once again, at dinner, she learns to be a winner.

"How are you my dear..." said Adroit, *"and how has been your day?"*

"Your words to me have been ecstatic..." said Gina, *"...and dad my day has been fantastic, but dad I'd like to hear some more, for tomorrow I'll be here no more"*

Amidst the biting, the chewing, the sipping and drinking, Adroit gave her new words for thinking.

"No matter whom you are: a person, it matters how you learn your lesson..." He said, *"...for having heard the voice of wisdom, you should also have a choice of kingdom"*

"Be a 'haver' my dear..." he continued, *"...for 'havers' never starve."* He spoke on, *"seven things that men must have and they will never starve. To have these seven things you must and your life will never rust,"*

To keep her life from future borrowing, he paused to see if she was following. Then he continued.

"VISION."

"Vision is the ability to see what others could not see"

"Make sure that you have a vision, for then, in life you'll have a mission; if your life has such direction; you can easily make a decision."

"COURAGE."

"Courage is the ability to act despite tremendous doubt."

"Take your time to build up courage; it will help put to work your knowledge. If you engage this entourage, you'll avoid life's demurrage."

"CREATIVITY."

"Creativity is the ability to think."

"Give your mind to creativity; you'll have a life of festivity.

If your mind, you cause to think, then in life you will not stink."

"TOLERANCE"

"Tolerance is the ability to understand criticism."

"There is no successful person that has never been criticized."

"Don't avoid taking criticism; but do avoid lurking pessimism. If you are not being criticized, you are not being utilized."

"DISCIPLINE"

"Discipline is the ability to delay gratification."

"Sorrow now and borrow never, or borrow now and sorrow ever: pay now; play later, or play now; pay later. Sacrifice short-term gain for long

term treasure: endure short-term pain for long-term pleasure. It can be difficult to deny short-term pleasure for long-term treasure-do it or it will 'do you.'"

"COMMITMENT"

"Commitment is the ability to continue walking even when nothing is working-getting yourself to a point of no return."

"In what you do be committed, from success you'll not be omitted. If you burn the bridge behind your back, you've torn the glitch that draws you back."

"PATIENCE"

"Patience is the ability to endure to success."

"Give yourself sometime to wait, having done all to change your fate, for while awaiting your change of state, your faith will make it worth the wait,"

"There my GINA, I've played my ace, now you're set to win the race. No matter what in life you face, never my dear diminish your pace,"

Adroit went on to take a nap; Gina went in to do a recap. Having gone through all as she read, she did retire to her bed.

CHAPTER FOUR

<u>FOUR PEOPLE TO KNOW</u>

*"...People who know.... shall prove themselves strong and shall stand firm and do exploits." **Dan 11:32 (AMP)***

JUANITA came home the previous night and heard the story of Gina's plight. Then deciding as mothers might, she gave to Gina broader sight.

"Come my daughter..." she said as to leave, Gina prepared.

"...to you my dear I have to show; the set of people you must know. If to you I this knowledge bestow, you'll know the places to cast your throw."

She held Gina's face between her palms, and looked at her with so much calm. She spoke to her with so much charm, her path to deliver from future harm.

"These four people you have to know; by this little knowledge you must grow."

"Know the one that you must follow; if you know him, you'll never sorrow"

"Know the one that you must enlighten; if you know him, your life will brighten"

"Know the one that you must avoid; if you know him, of problems you'll be devoid"

"Know the one that you must teach; if you know him, your dreams you'll reach,"

"Now I show you mind-boggling wisdom of how to know them with non-struggling freedom."

"LISTEN"

"He, who knows and knows he knows, is wise. FOLLOW HIM.

He, who knows and doesn't know he knows, is ignorant. ENLIGHTEN HIM.

He, who doesn't know and doesn't know he doesn't know, is a fool. AVOID HIM.

He, who doesn't know and knows he doesn't know, is a student. TEACH HIM,"

At this point, she fits the last pack of GINA's clothing in her little travel sack.

"There you are…" she said, "…my daughter, now your path is smooth as butter, if and only if you will trigger, every little wisdom, you'll grow bigger. Fare and farewell to a glorious future, go and never come back with a notorious suitor…" she smiled "…when next you come home on your closest recess, I pray we'll then hear of your choicest success. And err' we hear from you: from the horse's mouth; we should long have heard of you from the presses' shout,"

The driver drove our stirring Gina to the nearest airport. The next we got to hear of Gina was her success report.

CHAPTER FIVE

GINA'S SUCCESS

*"...that you may observe and do...and then you shall deal wisely and have good success." **JOSHUA 1:8 (AMP)***

Gina went on to succeed, and in though times didn't recede. She built herself a portfolio composition, which made her never compromise her position.

God and Gold and glory; what we heard as tabloids told her story. She made great wealth in dollars that it baffled, critics, called and callers,

She gave to every sphere, part of what she made to be their very own share. She built for many nations: Hotels, Houses....and Hospitals, and gave to vexed factions; wages, loans, donations...and capitals.

When asked on occasion, *"How can this great wealth be?"* she simply answered, *"Investment is the key."*

Once, someone said, *"Give truth to the erring youth!"* she said quite calmly,

"Listen today; glisten tomorrow: read today; lead tomorrow."

One day, JUANITA: her mother called on phone, and told her something that changed her life's tone,

"My dear baby..." she said *"...of your unending success we have heard, but lest your gladness to turned to madness, I've got this soundness to clear your blindness."*

Now Gina's heart began to pant, as these words JUANITA began to chant.

ZZ *"the greatest good we can do for others is not to share our riches with them but reveal their riches to them."*

She dropped the phone, the call to end, and Gina wisely, her life did mend. So one day, in a success seminar, millions did gather to hear this Gina. Watching them and seeing their longing, she gave to them her hearts belongings.

"I like the word investment..." she said, *"...it is a definite engagement: engaging the little you definitely have, to do the much you probably wouldn't have."*

"I took my father's words of wisdom, and ran my charted course with freedom; and not neglecting mother's knitted warnings, I tamed in me every heated yearning."

She glanced around the hall observing if her words they were reserving.

"I worked in places just like you do, but dealt with cases not like you would."

"For every kobo that I earned, I gave myself what I had gained. Ten percent of every cent, I kept at length not to be spent. And when some good books I had read, I then decided what should be bred. First I took my kobo gained and stored in a bank from whence it earned. I added more each time I earned and watched it grow as more it gained."

She paused and smiled wittingly.

"Investment..." she said nodding her head, *"...I like the word investment; it is a defined engagement. Invest your money and it will yield interest. Invest the interest and it will yield wealth"*

"I took my savings and made investment; I watched it gain as it brought repayment. I took the gain and reinvested; it brought me wealth, that's made you interested."

She climbed down the platform like an athlete in her top form; she then began to say some hidden truth as though it were forbidden fruit.

"Now I'm going to tell you..." she said, "...the little secret...of Gina's success"

"The secret is investment. There are two types of investment: direct investment and portfolio investment."

"DIRECT INVESTMENT"; "PORTFOLIO INVESTMENT"

"One should not be embarked upon without a very clear vision; the other should not be embarked upon without a clear decision."

"DIRECT INVESTMENT"

"It is investing in a vision; it is investment with a mission. It is investing in an idea, and it requires a lot of courage. My advice; don't launch into it, until you've succeeded in portfolio investment. It is investment that is big and risky, not to be compared with any brand of whisky. It is investment for the steady; don't go in till you are ready."

"PORTFOLIO INVESTMENT"

"It is investment that's virtually risk free, it is investing in another man's vision; it is investment without a mission. Invest in it even if you are not ready; when you are steady your yield will be ready."

"Five items make up the composition of what I call portfolio investment. They are;"

"MONEY MARKET, STOCK MARKET, REAL ESTATE, NETWORK MARKETING AND COMMODITIES."

"Invest in one, two...or better still all, but invest as much as your savings can take. When they yield, please reinvest, keep reinvesting until you are set. Before investing read about them, and while investing keep reading more. For when at last you are clear, you'll need the Knowledge to run your own. Take your yield to direct investment but don't discard your portfolio investment. Hand in hand they'll complement each other, for one is silver, and the other is gold. When eventually your direct investment becomes established, it will become another man's portfolio investment: it is a natural cycle."

And so did Gina speak, and much they did learn, when they had all gone, many their wealth did earn.

LAST WORDS

GINA'S PHILOSOPHICAL PRAISE

"In everything give thanks; for this is the will of God in Christ Jesus for you."
1THESS. 5:18 (NKJV)

The attitude of great gratitude is the aptitude for great altitude.

Gina knew this and would never forget, that thanking her parents, she'd

never regret.

Gina often called her folks and thanked them much for what they spoke.

One fine morning they got a parcel that came from Gina without a hassle.

In it contained a golden tablet, inscribed on it in diamond settings, the

following words,

THE GREATEST FOLKS ON EARTH

APOSTLE AND REV. MRS ADROITINCHRIST

WISDOM BLDG, WEALTH AVENUE

SUCCESS TOWN

NIGERIA.

Dear mummy and Daddy,

YOU STOOD TRUE

FAME: WHEN MY BLAZING SUN BURNED OUT

AND MY STRIKING HEIGHT GREW STOUT

WHEN MY FAME COULD PULL NO CLOUT

THEN YOUR WORD WON ME THE BOUT.

ABILITY: JUST AS ALL MY WALLS WENT DOWN

AND THE STORM WOULD MAKE ME DROWN

WHEN MY WEALTH COULD MAKE NO GOWN

THEN YOUR WORD BUILT ME A TOWN

INDEPENDENCE: WHEN ALL FRIENDS LEFT ME ALONE

AND MY FLUTE WOULD PLAY NO TONE

ALL MY SCIENCE COULD MAKE NO CLONE

THEN YOUR WORD GOT ME A PHONE

TEST: JUST AS I RESIGNED TO FATE

WITH ALL MY SPEED, STILL GOT THERE LATE

MY TIME MACHINE COULD FAKE NO DATE

YOUR WORD STOOD TRUE AND MADE ME GREAT

HONOUR: NOW I LOOK FROM SUCH GREAT HEIGHT

I SEE I WON THE VICTORY FIGHT

ALONE I COULD NOT SEE THIS LIGHT

YOU STOOD TRUE; WHAT GREAT DELIGHT.

Your loving daughter

GINA.